THERE WAS AN OLD LADY WHO SWALLOWED A ROSE!

by Lucille Colandro
Illustrated by Jared Lee

Cartwheel Books
an imprint of Scholastic Inc.

In loving memory of my mom and dad.
A special thank you to Mia.
— L.C.

To Lee and Beverly Dunn
— J.L.

ISBN 978-0-545-35223-9

Text copyright © 2012 by Lucille Colandro.
Illustrations copyright © 2012 by Jared D. Lee Studios.

12 11 10 9 8 7 6 5   13 14 15 16 17/0

Printed in the U.S.A.   40
First printing, November 2012

There was an old lady who swallowed a rose.
I don't know why she swallowed the rose,
but that's how it goes.

There was an old lady who swallowed some lace.
She didn't race to swallow that lace.

She swallowed the lace to tie to the rose.
I don't know why she swallowed the rose,
but that's how it goes.

There was an old lady who swallowed some glitter.
She wasn't a quitter to swallow the glitter.

She swallowed the glitter to trim the lace.
She swallowed the lace to tie to the rose.

I don't know why she swallowed the rose,
but that's how it goes.

There was an old lady who swallowed some candy.

It was fine and dandy to swallow that candy.

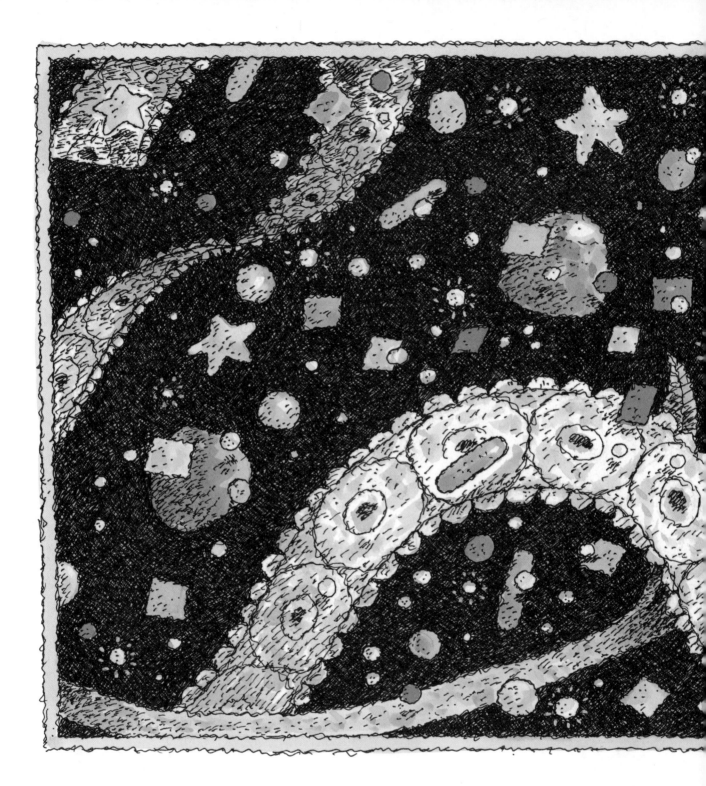

She swallowed the candy to garnish the glitter.
She swallowed the glitter to trim the lace.
She swallowed the lace to tie to the rose.

I don't know why she swallowed the rose,
but that's how it goes.

There was an old lady who swallowed a jewel.

She wasn't a fool to swallow that jewel.

She swallowed the jewel to brighten the candy.
She swallowed the candy to garnish the glitter.
She swallowed the glitter to trim the lace.

She swallowed the lace to tie to the rose.
I don't know why she swallowed the rose,
but that's how it goes.

There was an old lady who swallowed some hearts.
She showed her smarts by swallowing those hearts.

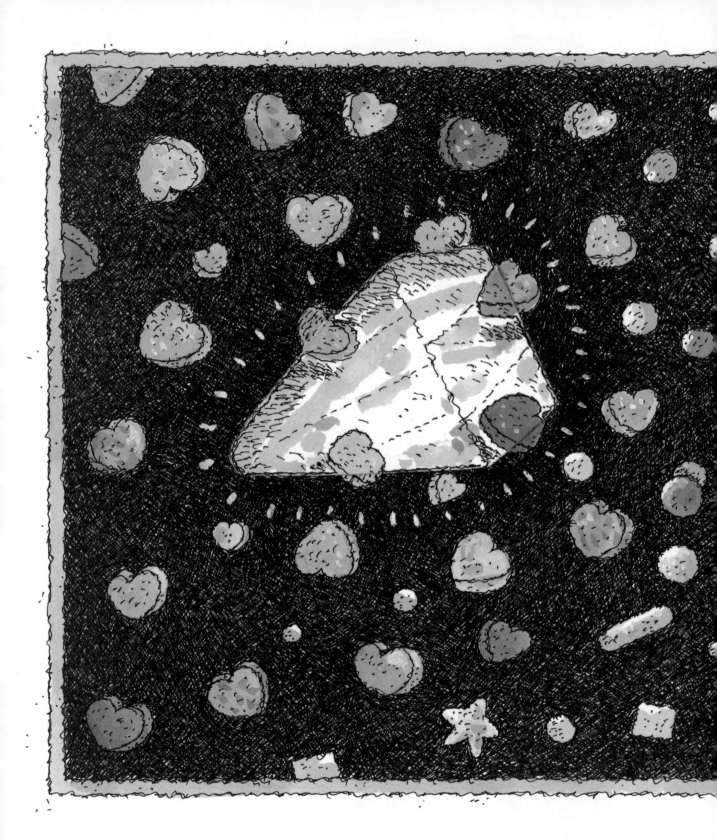

She swallowed the hearts to surround the jewel.

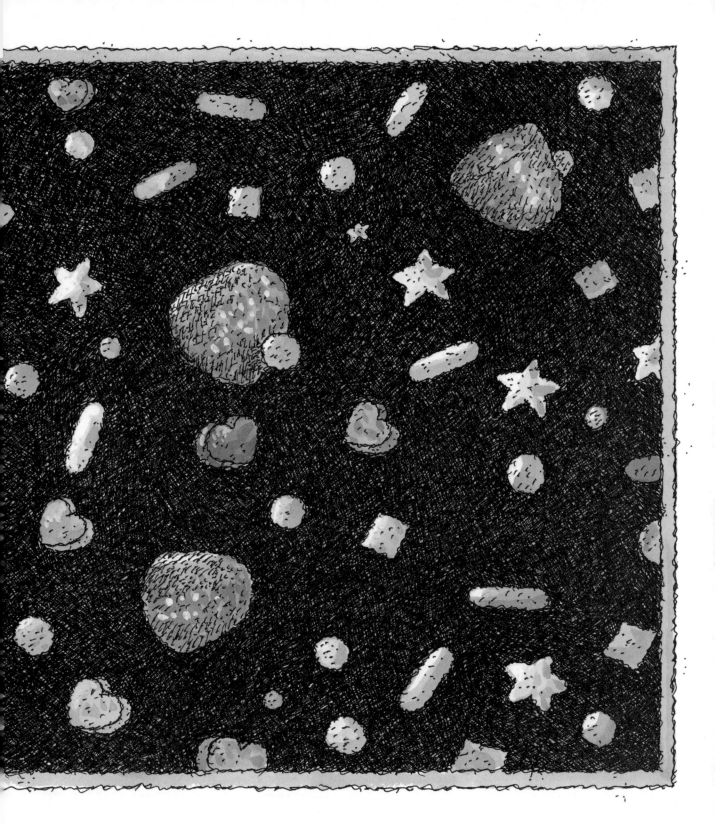

She swallowed the jewel to brighten the candy.

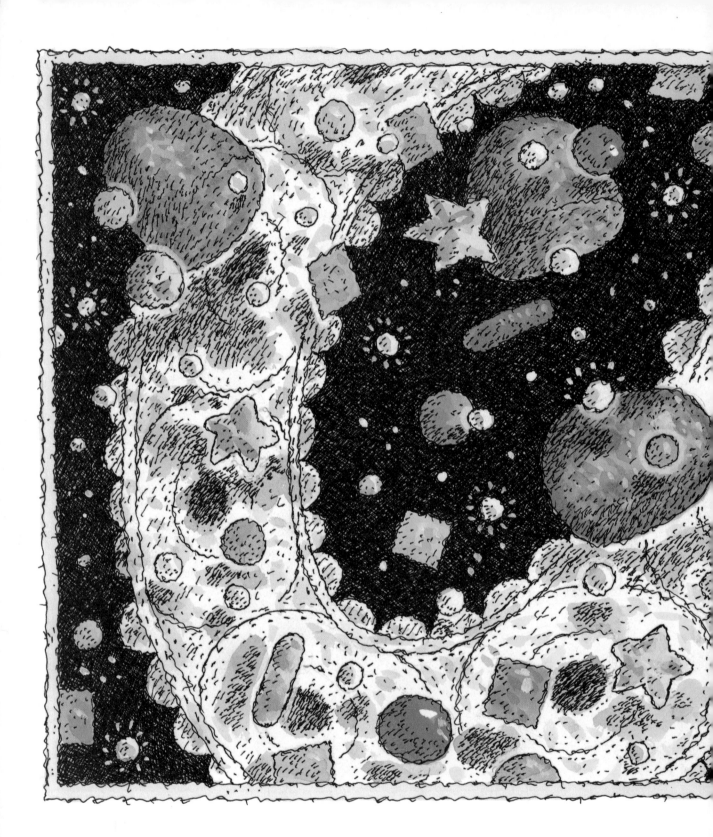

She swallowed the candy to garnish the glitter.

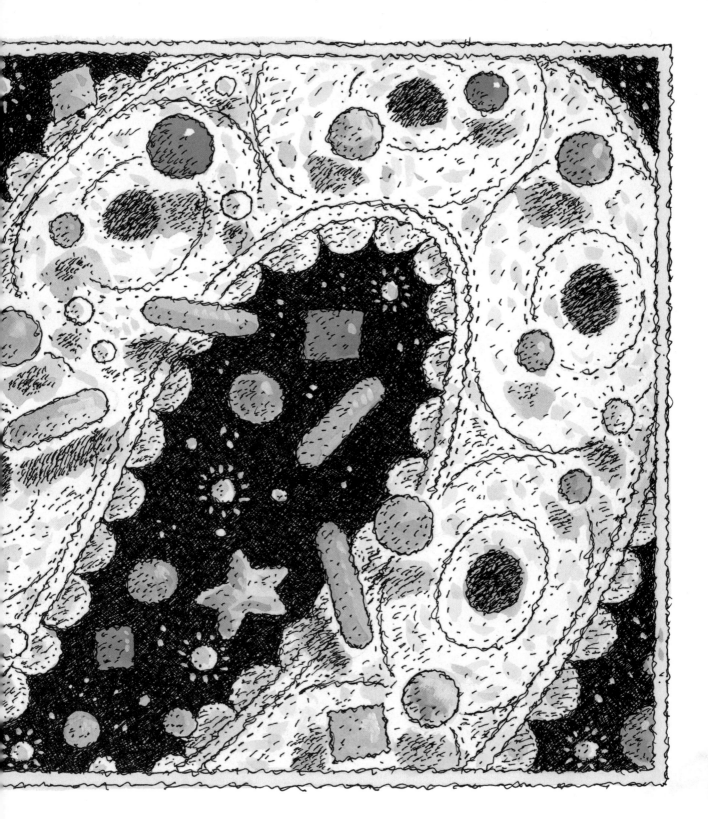

She swallowed the glitter to trim the lace.

She swallowed the lace to tie to the rose.

I don't know why she swallowed the rose,
but that's how it goes.

There was an old lady who swallowed a card.
It wasn't hard to swallow the card.

It brought the old lady so much happiness
that she smiled and laughed and . . .

. . . blew a big kiss!

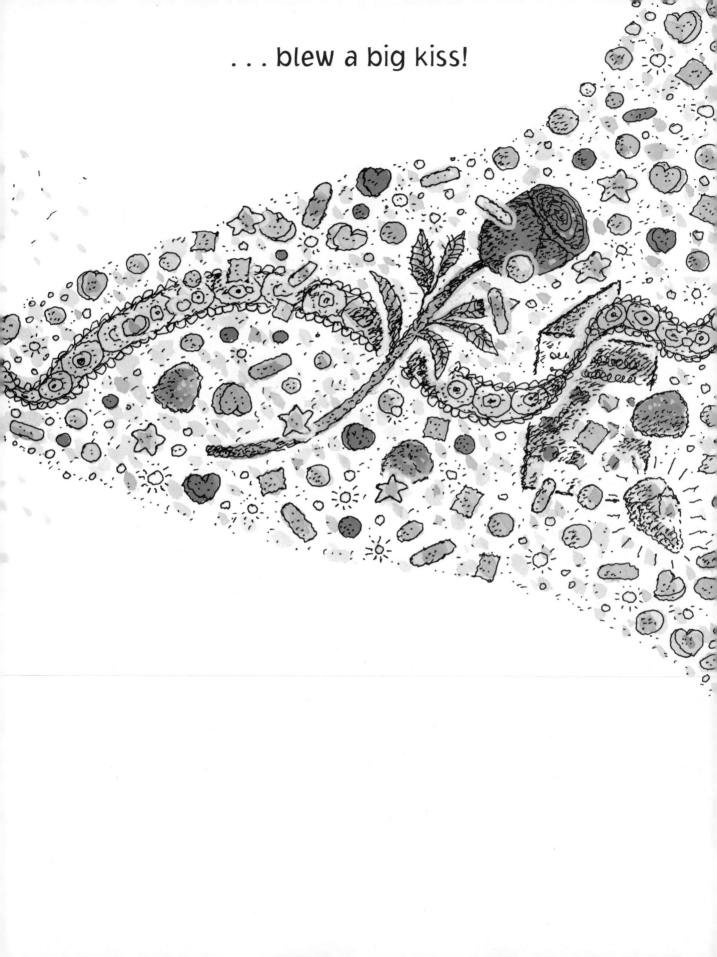

Happy Valentine's Day!